Look and Find®

P9-DCD-710

Disney

Tangled

publications international, ltd.
pi kids®

The King and Queen are thrilled to introduce their new baby. As they release a beautiful lantern in her honor, look around the plaza for these gifts the royal subjects have brought for the new princess.

When she was a baby, Rapunzel was stolen and locked in a tower by a mean and vain woman named Mother Gothel, who uses Rapunzel's magical hair to stay young. Since Rapunzel is never allowed outside the tower, she finds other ways to keep busy. Do you see some of her favorites?

Pottery

knitting needles

Darts

Book

Puzzle

Puppet

Guitar

Ballet shoes

Not too far from Rapunzel's tower, an outlaw named Flynn Rider hopes to escape capture. As Flynn attempts to outfox the captain's justice-loving horse, Maximus, look around the forest for these guards who'd be very happy to get their hands on him.

Rapunzel has persuaded Flynn Rider to take her to see the mysterious lanterns that always appear on her birthday. On the way, they've stopped at the Snuggly Duckling. There, they meet some ruffians with some surprising dreams. Can you find these thugs in the pub?

Ulf

Bartender

Killer

Attila

Hookhand

Tor

Bruiser

Rapunzel, Flynn, and their new friend, Maximus, have arrived in the town at last! Rapunzel has never seen anything like this. As she delights in all of the new experiences the town presents, look for these townspeople working hard to prepare for tonight's lantern festival.

Flynn shares a special moment with Rapunzel, but he's still a wanted man in the kingdom. As Rapunzel enjoys her first glimpse of the lanterns, scan the docks for these guards hoping to catch their man.

With the help of Maximus and the thugs, Flynn escaped from prison and is headed toward Rapunzel's tower...with the guards in hot pursuit. As the chase takes them across the kingdom, look for these items that have been mixed up in the chaos.

Basket

Bread

Milk

Boxes

Flag

Cart

Book

Laundry

Rapunzel couldn't be happier! Mother Gothel is gone, and she has finally returned to her parents, the King and Queen. As the kingdom celebrates Rapunzel's homecoming, search for these special presents her friends have brought to the party.

Flowers from Tor

Cupcake tower from Attila

Blanket sewn by Killer

Unicorn from Vladimir

Puppet from Fang

Sweater knitted by Bruiser

Every baby is special in its own way! Return to the plaza and look for these other babies.

Painting is Rapunzel's greatest joy. Climb back into the tower and look for these painting supplies.

Rapunzel hasn't had the opportunity to meet many of the forest's creatures. Gallop back to the woods and look for these animals she'll be very excited to see.

Rapunzel and Flynn never did get that bite to eat. Head back to the Snuggly Duckling and look for these meals they missed.

Snake-head soup

Putrified pudding

Phlegm stew

Chocolate-covered crickets

Hot-mess hash

Pickled chameleons

Moldy mudshake

Carcass casserole

Rapunzel discovered all kinds of new things in the town. Twirl back to the plaza preparations and look for these delicacies Rapunzel had never tried before.

Pudding

Carrot cake

Cupcake

Cheesecake

Eclair

Petits fours

Croissant

Row back to the harbor and count 20 purple lanterns.

Race back to the town and look for these guards trying to stop Flynn from escaping.

Waltz back to the plaza and look for these delighted guests celebrating Rapunzel's return.

Bartender

King and Queen

Hookhand

Maximus

Hair-braiding girl

Flag-selling boy